We Like Kids!

SONGBOOK

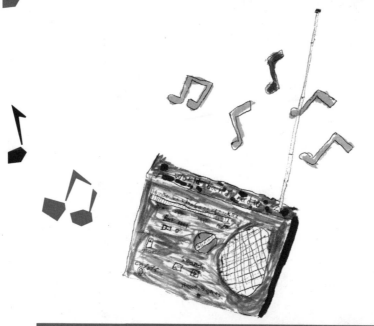

Compiled by Jeff Brown, Judy Hall, Jan Conitz

The Popular Syndicated Public Radio Program • KTOO-FM in Juneau, Alaska

GoodYearBooks

GoodYearBooks

are available for most basic curriculum subjects plus many enrichment areas. For more GoodYearBooks, contact your local bookseller or educational dealer. For a complete catalog with information about other GoodYearBooks, please write:

GoodYearBooks

ScottForesman
1900 East Lake Avenue
Glenview, IL 60025

ISBN 0-673-36038-5

1 2 3 4 5 6 7 8 9 - MAL - 00 99 98 97 96 95 94 93 92

 This book is printed on recycled paper.

Cover and title page illustrations by Breea DeSloover, Adam Lutchansky and Levi Preston.

An Introductory Word . . .

This is a collection of some of the best contemporary music for children.

As with most "adult" music, you'll find a variety of forms—rock, rap, and reggae, as well as some dynamite new "folk" songs for kids that are destined to become classics. You'll find songs by recognized "stars" in the children's music field, songs by folks you may not have known performed for children, and songs by performers you've never heard of before. Whomever they are, we know that you will be humming their tunes soon enough.

A few years back, children's music could be button-holed into a definite category. But one listen to music for kids today will astound any listener. It's the perfect marriage between a new generation of songwriters and modern recording technology, bringing to birth a wonderful cornucopia of voices, instruments, and styles.

Along with the increasing number of high-quality recordings for children, there has been an increase in the need for radio stations to program to listeners who place a value on raising our children with music that fosters a sense of self-respect, a love for ourselves as we are and others as they are, and a concern for the environment in which we live. That need is being met by over one hundred stations across the country who program music and/or stories for children. Many are locally originated programs hosted by volunteers.

You don't need a music degree to use this book. You'll find everything you need to start having fun right away: music, words, chords, and hints from the performers on playing the music with children. In the back of the book, you'll find information about the performers and a listing of addresses of handy resources.

As if that isn't enough, also included with the *WE LIKE KIDS! Songbook* is a cassette tape with all the great music you'll find in the songbook.

Have fun and learn the joys of music with the children you know!

Jeff, Judy, and Jan

About WE LIKE KIDS!

WE LIKE KIDS! is a weekly half-hour of songs and stories for kids of all ages. It is produced at public radio station KTOO-FM in Juneau, Alaska, and distributed free-of-charge to public radio stations over the National Public Radio satellite system. It's hosted by Alpine Annie (Judy Hall), Professor Sphagnum Moss (Jeff Brown), and Ramblin' Rose (Jan Conitz). They're assisted by a crew of kids and friends including, but not limited to: Leif, Rebecca, Sean, Patrice, Clarissa, Nathan, Beth, T. J., Lael, Clayton, Djuna, Marcus, Zeb, Randy, Odin, Gunnar, Cody, Sidra, Micah, Marlowe, Andrea, Colin, and Tugboat Tracy (Tracy Bird).

If your public radio station is not programming for children, give them a call. And while you're asking them to broadcast WE LIKE KIDS!, don't forget to ask how you can become a member of your community radio station.

Thanks!

We gratefully acknowledge the support of the many fine musicians whose work is included in the *WE LIKE KIDS! Songbook.* Without exception, each has donated their share of the royalties to the production and distribution of WE LIKE KIDS! Without the generosity of all, this project would not have been possible.

Additional folks who provided invaluable help were Robert Cohen, Mike Sakarias, P. J. Swift, Tom Nieman, Bill Legere, Peter Frid, Cherry Lane Music, The Children's Group, Rounder Records, Music for Little People, A Gentle Wind, Maureen Conerton, Laurell Clough, and Billy Hudson.

Special thanks also go to Lynne Grenier, graphic design, and Lois Eve Anderson, music notation.

Contents

Song		Page
Annie, My Cooking Friend	Ella Jenkins	1
Away, Mommy, Away	Timmy Abell	4
Beans for Brunch	Jory	6
Bubble with Your Goldfish	Jim Valley	8
Chickens in My Hair	Willie Sterba	12
Come On and Sing Along	Tom Callinan	14
Costume Party	Peter Alsop	16
Daddy, Won'tcha Come Out and Fish with Me?	Eric Hummel and Peggy Hovik	18
50 Ways to Fool Your Mother	Bill Harley	20
Fishy Doo-Ah	Nancy Tucker	22
Going to the Zoo	Tom Paxton	25
Goodnight	Saragail Katzman	27
Handyman	Marc and Carol Finkelstein	28
The Harmony Song	The Chenille Sisters	30
I Am Who I Am	Lois LaFond	32
I Wanna Try It	Peter Alsop	34
I Wonder Where's My Underwears	Peanutbutterjam	36
The Kid Who Got Lost in the Blanket Toss	J. D. Uponen and Lori Pleshe	37
Little Hands	Jonathan Edwards	40
The Marvelous Toy	Tom Paxton	42
Moose on the Loose	Carol Lavrakas	44
My Sister's a Whale in the Sea	The Singing Rainbows	46
Nobody Else Like Me	Mary Lu Walker	48
Oh No! I Like My Sister!	Barry Louis Polisar	50
Read a Book	Cathy Fink and Marcy Marxer	52
Simple Thing	Kim & Jerry Brodey	54
Teaching Peace	Red Grammer	56
Tick Tock	Linda Arnold	58
The Walrus LIfe	Bill Wellington	61
What Happened to the Dinosaurs?	Paul Strausman	63
The World Is a Rainbow	Greg and Steve	65
About The Artists		69
Resources		81

Annie, My Cooking Friend

words and music by Ella Jenkins

An- nie, (An- nie), cook me some long string beans, (cook me some

long string beans.) An- nie, (An- nie), cook me some

mus- tard greens, (cook me some mus- tard greens). An- nie,

(An- nie), would you kind- ly please? (would you kind- ly please?)

Annie, (Annie), cook me some black- eyed peas, (cook me some

black- eyed peas). An- nie, (An- nie), did you

hear what I said? (Did you hear what I said?) An- nie,

(An- nie), I'd like some hot corn bread. (I'd like some hot corn bread).

Annie, (Annie), is my cook- ing friend, (is my

cook- ing friend). An- nie, (An- nie), I'd

sure like to taste, (I'd sure like to taste), your good cook- ing a- gain

(your good cook- ing a- gain...) mmm mmm mmm mmm mmm

Fine

mmmmmmmmmmmmmmmm . . .

Away, Mommy, Away

words and music by Timmy Abell

1. We'-re   bound for the   bath- tub, we're   bound to get   wet.
2.   day   in the   dirt   and the   grease and the sand.

A- way,   Mom- my, a- way, a- way. We've got to get scrubbed and then
A- way,   Mom- my, a- way, a- way. A   sail- in' we'll go, it's good-

off to our beds.   Mom- my, we're   bound a- way.   It's all   way.
bye to dry land.   Mom- my, we're   bound a- way.   Well, haul

3. Well, haul off your clothes and hop into the tub.
   Away, Mommy, away, away.
   Hold fast to that washcloth and give a good rub.
   Mommy, we're bound away.

4. Well, I've got me a toy boat and a squirt gun or two.
   Away, Mommy, away, away.
   And a "bottle o' suds" for each of the crew.
   Mommy, we're bound away.

5. Well, the sailing is fine, and the weather is clear.
   Away, Mommy, away, away.
   Now look who comes in and starts scrubbing our hair.
   Mommy, please go away.

6. Now the tide it is running away down the drain.
   Away, Mommy, away, away.
   The water's all sudsy and we are all clean.
   Mommy, we're bound away.

7. So pull down the sheets and make ready for bed.
   Away, Mommy, away, away.
   It's "anchors a' weigh" now for this sleepy head.
   Mommy, we're bound away.

Beans for Brunch

words and music by Jory Aronson

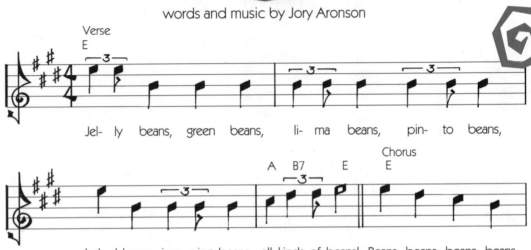

Jel- ly beans, green beans, li- ma beans, pin- to beans,

baked beans, jum- ping beans, all kinds of beans! Beans, beans, beans, beans,

beans, beans, beans, beans, beans, beans, beans, beans, all kinds of beans!

Beans for din- ner, beans for lunch, beans for break- fast, beans for brunch!

Pork and beans, string beans, cof- fee beans, Na- vy beans, kid- ney beans, pole

all kinds of beans! Beans, beans, beans, beans, beans, beans, beans, beans,

beans, beans, beans, beans, all kinds of beans! Beans for dinner, beans for lunch,

beans for break- fast, beans for brunch! Bush beans, snap beans, soy beans, wax beans,

run- ner beans, fa- va beans, all kinds of beans! Beans, beans, beans, beans,

beans, beans, beans, beans, beans, beans, beans, beans, all kinds of beans!

Beans for din- ner, beans for lunch, beans for break- fast, beans for brunch!

Bubble with Your Goldfish

words by Kitty Danziero's Fourth-Grade Class • Daffodil Valley Elementary, Sumner, Washington • music by Jim Valley

Laugh with your cat!   (Laugh with your cat!)   Grin with your dog!

(Grin with your dog!) Bub- ble with your gold- fish! (Bub- ble with your gold- fish!)

Kiss a bull- frog!   (Kiss a bull- frog!)   Sing with the flow- ers!

(Sing with the flow- ers!) Play some games! (Play some games!) Sit by the fire and

lis- ten to the flames.   Sit by the fire and   lis- ten to the flames!

Smile at the peo- ple go- in' down your street!

(REPEAT CHORUS) In- vite your neigh- bors to

have some tea. Grin and chuck- le, it's all for free!

Help a gran- ny to cross the street, on the bus, give her your seat.

(REPEAT CHORUS) Go up to your girl- friend, give her a wink,

write her a let- ter in rain- bow ink! Wish up- on a star,

wish up-on a moon.   Watch out! You'll   be   laugh-in' soon!

(REPEAT CHORUS)   Sit by the fire and   lis-ten to the flames.

Sit by the fire and   lis-ten to the flames.

Chickens in My Hair

words and music by Willie Sterba

Chorus
(capo up 5 frets)

Chick- ens, chick- ens in my hair. I've got chick- ens ev- 'ry- where.

Some are here and some are there, oh chick- ens ev- 'ry- where. 1. I

Verse

2. I

1. bought a love- ly chick- en to bring home to my wife. And
2. gave them toast for break- fast. I could- n't serve them eggs. When

1. on that ve- ry morn- ing, my life turned in- to strife. The
2. we got through, I said, "Oh whew! I am on my last legs." And

1. chick- ens had ten cous- ins and each one had a niece. They
2. then there came a knock- ing, a knock- ing at the door. I

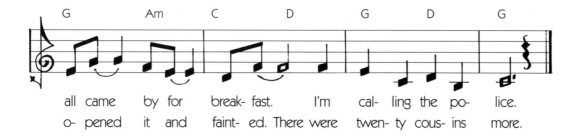

G	Am	C	D	G	D	G

all came   by for   break- fast.   I'm   cal- ling the po-   lice.
o- pened   it and   faint- ed. There were   twen- ty cous- ins   more.

3. The cousins came to visit, and then they stayed for lunch.
   I almost lost my hearing, when they began to munch.
   My poor wife started crying, the chickens they were flying,
   I thought that I was dying—and then there came a knock.

4. The door I opened slowly, and much to my surprise,
   A hundred chickens standing there, a-looking at my eyes.
   The first one had an envelope, and handed it to me.
   The invitation inside read, "Come here, the food is free."

5. Now dinnertime was coming, so I sat them in a group.
   I told them they could stay and have my scrumptious
   chicken soup.
   Well, they clucked and scrambled for the door,
   and in a minute flat,
   I had no chickens anywhere.
   Now what'd ya think of that?

   Well, I had chickens in my hair
   Had those chickens everywhere
   Had some here and had some there
   Had chickens everywhere.

   Now I have no chickens anywhere,
   Have no chickens in my hair,
   Not one here, and not one there,
   No chickens anywhere.

Luke Boyles

Come On and Sing Along

words and music by Tom Callinan

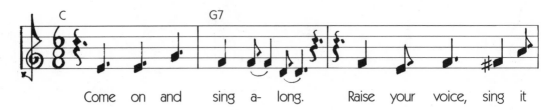

Come on and sing a- long. Raise your voice, sing it

loud and strong. There ain't no way you can do it wrong if you

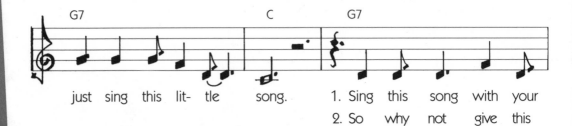

just sing this lit- tle song. 1. Sing this song with your
2. So why not give this

Mom and Dad. Sing this song if you're feel- ing mad.
song a try? It just might dry those tears from your eye.

Sing   this song if you're   kind of   blue   'cause it
The young can sing it   with the old ones too, 'cause when

just   might help you for- get   what's troub-   lin' you.
you're old   some day, some kid   might sing this song with you.

3. So put your arm around the person there
   Whether bald or grey or with short or long hair.
   What matters is what's in their heart.
   So come everybody, sing your part!

4. So as through life you go,
   When you're high and when you're low,
   Even if you are in pain,
   Try to rise above it, sing this chorus again!

Costume Party

words and music by Peter Alsop

It's a cos- tume par- ty, and ev- 'ry- one is here.

It's a cos- tume par- ty, and ev- 'ry- one is here.

1. You wear a blue dress, you, red sneak- ers, you wear a suit and tie.
2. You wear brown skin, you wear white, your head is clean and bare.

You wear flow- ers. You wear stripes. You put
You poked holes through your ear- lobes. You got a

make- up on your eyes. It's a wart, I bet some- where! or
wheels when we walk. It's a

may- be you dye your hair!? It's a who we are in- side!

D.C. al fine

It's a

3. We may be blind, or
   We wear glasses
   We st-stutter when we talk
   Sometimes our ears
   Just do not hear
   Or we use wheels when we walk!

4. Our disguises
   Could win prizes
   Each one's qualified.
   But the only thing
   That really matters
   Is who we are inside!

Julia Cohen

Daddy, Won'tcha Come Out and Fish with Me?

words and music by Eric Hummel

Chorus

Dad- dy won'tcha come out, Dad- dy won't- cha come out, Dad-

dy won't- cha come out and fish with me? I want to catch him

all a- lone. Show him to my friends when I get home.

Verse

1. Dad- dy won't- cha come out and fish with me? I
2. I know there's a hal-i- - but wait- ing out there.

know there's a big one just wait- ing for me. Dad- dy please get out my
Just a- bout as big as a gri- zz- ly bear. He's so big I can't

fi- shing pole. I just want to catch a fi- let of sole.
pull him in. More than se- ven feet from fin to fin.

3. Pull out of the harbor at a quarter to eight.
   Fish are biting and I hope we're not late.
   Cruisin' through the narrows on a sunny day.
   Around the point to Vallenar Bay.

4. We're on the grounds at half past eight.
   Hook on the bottom with octopus bait.
   Nibble on the hook and a tug on the line.
   I think we got a big fish this time.

5. I reel him in, then he takes a run.
   I can't remember when I had so much fun.
   Daddy, please help me, my fingers are sore.
   But in three seconds flat, I'll be ready for more.

6. He runs back and forth all over the place.
   Once he comes up and I can see his face.
   He's big and he's ugly, he's scary and mean.
   He's the biggest fish that I've ever seen.

7. He finally gets tired and we bring him to
   the top.
   My daddy takes a baseball bat and gives
   him a whop.
   We hoist him on the deck and we hang him
   from the scale.
   Daddy says he's bigger than a humpback
   whale.

8. We take him home to Mommy and she
   thinks it's great.
   She says I'm the best fisherperson in the
   state.
   And then I have to clean him and that's not
   a pretty sight.
   So I'll tell you about it another night.

50 Ways to Fool Your Mother

words and music by Bill Harley

Early in the morning when you open up your eyes
You can hear the coffee perking and the egg your mother fries
Lyin' in your bed, you start to feel blue
When you think of all the things that you really want to do.

You want to play baseball, you want to ride your bike,
You want to read a comic book, you want to take a hike.
But no you don't, there's something else to do.
Dress yourself and have your breakfast, you've got to go to school.
If just this once you didn't have to go
But if you ask, they'll just say no.
If you only think a moment, there's something you can do.
There must be 50 ways to fool your mother,
50 ways to fool your mother.

It's really rather simple if you only stop and think.
You could tell her you got sick last night and threw up in the sink.
Say you got the measles, say you got the mumps,
Tell her that you're too depressed and way down in the dumps.
Say that you're not you, there's a Martian in your place.
You're really on a rocket ship somewhere in outer space.
Oh you've got to use your head, but I'm sure you'll find a way.
There must be 50 ways to fool your mother,
50 ways to fool your mother.

You could tell her that your teacher said you've done so well
You don't have to go to school today, you can rest a spell.
Tell her that a tidal wave is comin' to your town.
If you try to get to school, you just might drown.
Say a herd of elephants is roamin' through the streets,
That your shoes have shrunk, they won't fit on your feet.
Say your school was zapped into hyperspace.
There must be 50 ways to fool your mother,
50 ways to fool your mother.

You could tell her that your turtle's sick, you've got to stay at home.
You're waiting for the President to call you on the phone.
Say you're sore and achy, there's a pounding in your head,
That your legs won't move, you can't get out of bed.
Tell her that you won't get up, you know it's just a dream.
You know your real mother would never act so mean.
Put some powder on your face until it's really white.
Heat up the thermometer over the light.
Take some iodine and put some spots upon your face.
There must be 50 ways to fool your mother,
50 ways to fool your mother.

So your mother finally buys it and says "OK,
But if you're so sick, you can't go out to play.
You've got to stay at home, you've got to get some rest.
I can help you with your homework, you can study for your test.
Maybe by tomorrow you'll feel OK,
I'm really very sorry that you're sick on Saturday."
SATURDAY! I didn't know it was Saturday!

Your mother smiles sweetly as she gets up to leave.
You should have known that mothers got something up their sleeves.

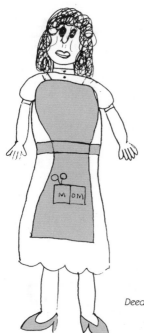

There must be some way out of this,
something you can do.
Are there 50 more ways to fool your mother?
50 ways to fool your mother?
50 ways to fool your mother?

Deedra M. Kinerk

Fishy Doo-ah

words and music by Nancy Tucker

Look- in' at fish- ies like flow- ers with fins (Fish- y doo- ah,

fish- y doo- ah). A- lum- i- num foil fish with- out an- y chins.

(Fish- y doo- ah, fish- y doo- ah, doo- ah). Fish with lips turned

up in grins, are puck- er- ing proud look- in' down at all the

plaid clad peo- ple... with- out an- y fins (Peo- ple doo- ah,

peo- ple doo- ah). Red swea- ter peo- ple... with long hai- ry chins

(Peo- ple doo- ah, peo- ple doo- ah, doo- ah). Col- or- ful peo- ple look- in'

in with grins, fish look- in' out while we're look- in' in.

May- be we're all in a- qua- ri- ums

(A- qua- ri- um doo- ah, a- qua- ri- um doo- ah),

theirs made of wa- ter... and ours made of air.

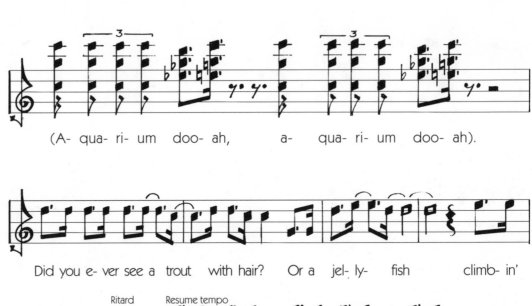

(A- qua- ri- um doo- ah, a- qua- ri- um doo- ah).

Did you e- ver see a trout with hair? Or a jel- ly- fish climb- in'

Ritard   **Resume tempo**

up the stairs?   Stick- y doo- ah, stick- y doo- ah, doo- ah eeooooh...

Ann Boyles

Goin' to the Zoo

words and music by Tom Paxton

Moderately fast

1. Dad- dy's tak- ing us to the zoo to- mor- row,
2. See the e- le- phant with the long trunk swing- in',

zoo to- mor- row, zoo to- mor- row. Dad- dy's tak- ing us to the
great big ears and long trunk swing- in'. Snif- fin' up pea- nuts with the

zoo to- mor- row; we can stay all day. We're go- ing to the zoo, zoo,
long trunk swing- in', we can stay all day. We're go- ing to the zoo, zoo,

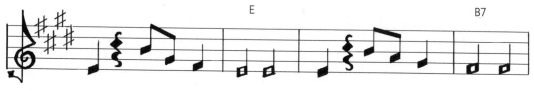

zoo; how a- bout you, you, you? You can come too, too,
zoo; how a- bout you, you, you? You can come too, too,

We Like Kids! Songbook

Julia Cohen

too. We're go- ing to the zoo, zoo, zoo. We're go- ing to the
too. We're go- ing to the zoo, zoo, zoo.

zoo, zoo, zoo; how a- bout you, you, you? You can come

too, too, too; we're go- ing to the zoo, zoo, zoo.

3. See all the monkeys scritch scritch scratchin'
   Jumpin' all around and scritch scritch
   scratchin',
   Hangin' by their long tails, scritch scritch
   scratchin'
   We can stay all day. *(To chorus)*

4. Big black bear all huff huff a-puffin',
   Coat's too heavy, he's huff huff a-puffin',
   Don't get too near the huff huff a-puffin'
   Or you won't stay all day. *(To chorus)*

5. Seals in the big pool all honk honk honkin'
   Catchin' fish and honk honk honkin'
   Little seals honk honk honkin'
   (high pitched voice)
   We can stay all day. *(To chorus)*

6. *(slower tempo)*
   We stayed all day and we're gettin' sleepy
   Sittin' in the car gettin' sleep sleep sleepy.
   Home already and we're sleep sleep sleepy.
   We have stayed all day. *(To chorus)*

CHORUS
   We've been to the zoo, zoo, zoo.
   So have you, you, you.
   You can come too, too, too.
   We've been to the zoo, zoo, zoo.

7. Momma's taking us to the zoo tomorrow,
   Zoo tomorrow, zoo tomorrow.
   Momma's taking us to the zoo tomorrow,
   We can stay all day. *(To chorus)*

Julia Cohen

Goodnight

words and music by Saragail Katzman

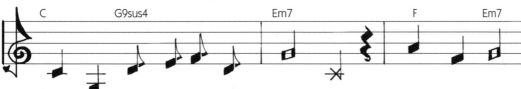

1. A mouse goes squeak and says good night. Squeak! A
2. An owl goes whoo and says good night. Whoo! An

mouse goes squeak and says sleep tight. Squeak! Squeak, good night!
owl says whoo and says sleep tight. Whoo! Whoo, good night

Squeak, sleep tight. Squeak, good night to the chil- dren. An
Whoo, sleep tight. Whoo, good night to the chil- dren. The

3. The wind goes whoosh,
and says good night.
Whoosh!
The wind goes whoosh,
And says sleep tight,
Whoosh, goodnight,
Whoosh, sleep tight.
Whoosh, good night
To the children.

4. The stars go
Twinkling good night.
Twinkle!
The stars go
Twinkling sleep tight.
Twinkle, good night,
Twinkle, sleep tight.
Twinkle, good night
To the children.

Handyman

words and music by Marc D. Finkelstein and Carol W. Finkelstein

1. Chomp, chomp, chomp, I'm a croc- o- di- le.
2. Wiggle, wiggle, wiggle, I'm a wiggle bun- ny. I

Chomp, chomp, chomp, I chomp and then I smi- le.
wiggle my ears, I wig- gle them fun- ny.

Chomp, chomp, chomp, I'm a croc- o- di- le. Chomp!
Wiggle, wiggle, wiggle, I'm a wig- gle bun- ny. Wiggle!

I'm a han- dy- man, work- ing with my hands.

Colin Connerton

G7　　　　　　　　　　　　　　　　　　　Emin7

Mak- ing　han- dy　friends,　　　my work　ne- ver ends.

1.-5.　　6.-7.
A7sus　　A7sus　　　D.S. and fade

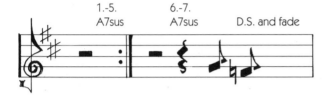

I'm　a

3.　Gobble, gobble, gobble, I'm a gobble turkey.
　　Gobble, gobble, gobble, I gobble and I'm jerky.
　　Gobble, gobble, gobble, I'm a gobble turkey.
　　Gobble, gobble, gobble!

CHORUS

4.　Creep, creep, creep, I'm a creeping spider.
　　Creep, creep, creep, always creeping higher.
　　Creep, creep, creep, I'm a creeping spider.
　　Creep!

CHORUS

5.　Hiss, hiss, hiss, I'm a sliding snake.
　　Hiss, hiss, hiss, is the sound I make.
　　Hiss, hiss, hiss, I'm a sliding snake.
　　Hiss!

CHORUS

6.　Gonna swim, swim, swim, I'm a sea turtle.
　　Swim, swim, swim, gliding over hurdles.
　　Swim, swim, swim, I'm a sea turtle.
　　Watch me swim, do the swim, like her, like him!

CHORUS

The Harmony Song

words and music by Connie Huber and Grace Morand

You can sing a- ny- where, e- ven all a- lone.

You can sing out- side, and when you're at home.

You can sing with your friends and ea- si- ly,

sing diff- erent things and make har- mon- y.

1. I sing the mel- o- dy, and I sing the har- mon- y, and
2. I sing the mel- o- dy, and we sing the har- mon- y, and

(Second verse to Coda)

when we sing to- geth- er, it   sounds just right to me.
when we sing to- geth- er, it   sounds just right for three.

I'd like to sing with you.   There can be more than two.

I like to sing up high, it   sounds like some- thing new.

(Repeat each set of measures and then sing all together)

La, la, la, la,   la, la, la.   La, la, la, la,

la, la, la.   La, la, la, la,   la, la, la.

I Am Who I Am!

words and music by Lois LaFond

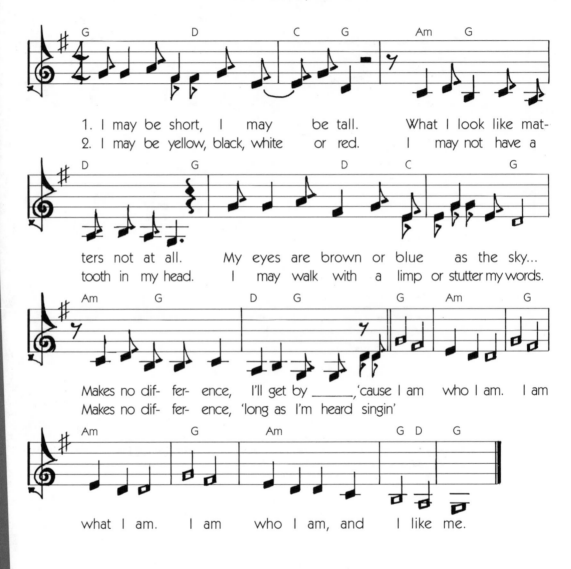

1. I may be short, I may be tall. What I look like mat-
2. I may be yellow, black, white or red. I may not have a

ters not at all. My eyes are brown or blue as the sky...
tooth in my head. I may walk with a limp or stutter my words.

Makes no dif- fer- ence, I'll get by _____, 'cause I am who I am. I am
Makes no dif- fer- ence, 'long as I'm heard singin'

what I am. I am who I am, and I like me.

3. I may speak words you don't understand.
    I may eat food with the other hand.
    Every girl and boy is a special one.
    We're each so different and that's more fun, 'cause

    I am who I am.
    I am what I am.
    I am who I am.
    And I like me!

    You are who you are.
    You are what you are.
    You are who you are and
    I like you!

    Oh, we are who we are.
    We are what we are.
    We are who we are and
    I like everybody!

I Wanna Try It

words and music by Peter Alsop

Reggae
Chorus

I wan- na try it. I wan- na try it. Give me a chance to learn.

I wan- na try it. I wan- na try it. It's my turn.

Verse

1. My dad bought a toy for me. He
2. My grand- ma said she'd teach me how to

o- pened up the box. He read di- rec- tions.
bake a cake with her. But she did ev- 'ry

1., 2.

set it up. Then he broke it while I watched. Not again, Dad!
thing her- self. And she'd on- ly let me stir. Awww Grand- ma!

more! Yeah! 4. My sis- ter says that math is ea- sy. She
stuff, yeah! 6. I al- read- y watched you do it, and

says, "It's real- ly fun!" She helped me with my home-
I sat pa- tient- ly. I know I can

work prob- lems, but she fin- ished ev- 'ry one. That's okay. but
do it now, c'mon and hand it o- ver to me!

Eh- eh, Eh- eh! It's my turn! It's my turn!

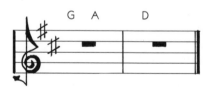

3. Sometimes I do jigsaw puzzles,
   All spread out on the floor.
   My mom comes, finds all the pieces.
   Then it's fun no more! Yeah!

5. I'm too young or I'm too little,
   Or I'm not strong enough!
   What I am is tired of watching
   You guys do my stuff, yeah!

I Wonder Where's My Underwears

words and music by Eileen Packard

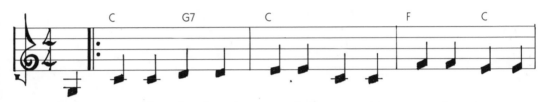

I won- der where's my un- der- wears, my un- der- wears so

fine. Oh, are they in the wash- er, where's those un- der- wears of

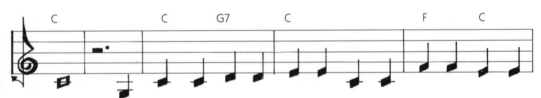

mine! 1. Say are they in the bur- eau drawer, or un- der- neath my
2. I asked my mom where they might be, I al- so asked my

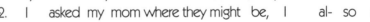

bed? Did my bro- ther take them now, and put them on his head? I
dad. They were my favor- ite un- der- wears, the best ones that I had. Well,

3. Well, are they on the clothesline?
   Did they blow into a tree?
   I have to find those underwears!
   Oh gosh—oh, golly gee!

CHORUS

4. Did they get lost among the rags,
   Or has my puppy got 'em?
   Hey—Look, I found my underwears!
   They're right here on my bottom!

CHORUS

The Kid Who Was Lost (On the Blanket Toss)

words and music by J. D. Uponen

1. They were hav- ing the u- su- al fun, and the
2. real- ly con- fused as to why, the kid

fes- ti- val had just be- gun. The Es- ki- mos came in for
ne- ver came down from the sky. Some Es- ki- mos thought he looked

miles to cel- e- brate spring for a while; They
good to an ea- gle out search- ing for food; some

star- ted by sing- ing the songs the el- ders all played on their
o- thers thought may- be a breeze took him out to the Ber- ing

drums.   The   next e- vent   was   when   it   hap- pened: the
Sea.   May- be it could   if   it   filled   the   hood   of the

kid was lost   on   the   blan- ket toss!   It's so hard to be- lieve
kid who was lost on the   blan- ket toss!

(It's so hard to be- lieve.)   It could pos- si- bly be   (It could pos- si- bly be)

He was up in the air   (He was up in the air)   Then he was- n't there

(Then he was- n't there)   They looked on the ground   (They looked on the ground)

They looked all a- round   (They looked all a- round)   The kid, he was lost

(The kid, he was lost) on the blan- ket toss. (on the blan- ket toss!)

They were toss. a- bout toss (the kid, he was lost)

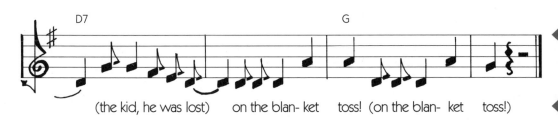

(the kid, he was lost) on the blan- ket toss! (on the blan- ket toss!)

3. Seven months after that night,
    The kid came into town all right.
    The Eskimos came into town
    To see how that kid had came down.
    He said, "You threw me so hard that ca-pow!
    I went into space and that's how,
    The Eskimos got the first astronaut."
    The kid who was lost
    on the blanket toss!

Deedra Kinerk

Little Hands

words and music by Jonathan Edwards

(Capo up two frets)

1. Look at those hands, those ba- by's hands, dim- pled and fat like a

pil- low. May they grow up to be as strong as an oak

and as grace- ful as a wil- low. 2. Oh lord, what will they do, I'm

ask- in' you, will they bake bread or play the fid- dle?

For all I know they will build a new world, while mine grow old and

brit- tle.   Lit- tle   hands, lit- tle   hands,   what are

you gon- na do?   To-   day you be- long to a   ba- by, to-

mor- row you'll be-   long   to a   la- dy.   3. I

love you lit-   tle hands,   when you're   play- in' in the sand,

and the way you love your   mo- ther.   I will hold on to the mem-

'ry of this scene,   like one hand holds the   o- ther.

The Marvelous Toy

words and music by Tom Paxton

Moderate tempo

1. When I was just a wee lit- tle lad, full of health and
2. (The) first time that I picked it up, I had a big sur-

joy, my fa- ther home- ward came one night, and gave to me a
prise, for right on its bottom were two big buttons that looked like big green

toy. A won- der to be- hold it was, with man- y col- ors
eyes. I first pushed one and then the other, and then I twisted its

bright. And the mo- ment I laid eyes on it, it be-
lid. And when I set it down a- gain,

came my heart's de- light. It went "Zip" when it moved, and
here is what it did: It still goes "Zip" when it moves, and

"Bop" when it stopped, and "Whirr" when it stood still. I nev- er knew just
"Bop" when it stops, and "Whirr" when it stands still. I nev- er knew just

what it was, and I guess I nev- er will. The will.
what it was, and I guess I nev- er will. It

3.   It first marched left and then marched right,
And then marched under a chair.
And when I looked where it had gone,
It wasn't even there!
I started to sob, then my daddy laughed.
For he knew that I would find,
When I turned around, my marvelous toy,
Chugging from behind!

CHORUS

4. Well, the years have gone by too quickly it seems,
And I have my own little boy,
And yesterday I gave to him
My marvelous little toy.
His eyes nearly popped right out
of his head,
And he gave a squeal of glee,
Neither one of us knows just what it is,
But he loves it just like me.

CHORUS

Moose on the Loose
(Riding Alaska's Train)

words and music by Carol Lavrakas

Start slowly

All a- board! There's a moose on the loose, in the ca- boose
There's a seal with an eel, eat- ing corn meal

A7   D

rid- ing A- las- ka's Train. There's a bear back there in his
rid- ing A- las- ka's Train. There's an otter in the wa- ter

A7   D   D

un- der wear rid- ing A- las- ka's Train. Rid- ing the train
doin' what he oughter rid- ing A- las- ka's Train.

G   D   A7   D   D

rid- ing the train rid- ing A- las- ka's Train. Rid- ing the train through the

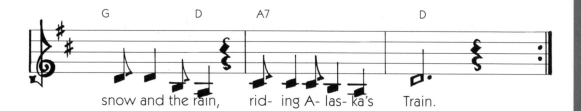

snow and the rain,   rid- ing A- las- ka's   Train.

(Modulate to E)

3. There's a whale with his tail—
    stuck in a pail,
    Riding Alaska's Train.
    There's a caribou—who lost his shoe,
    Riding Alaska's Train.

4. There's a duck who's stuck—
    in a red truck,
    Riding Alaska's Train.
    There's a reindeer—looking in the mirror.
    Riding Alaska's Train.

CHORUS

(Start to slow rhythm/Modulate to F#)

5. There's a porcupine—
    standing in line,
    Riding Alaska's Train.
    There's a crow—don't you know—
    waiting to go,
    Riding Alaska's Train.
    (End with
    "CHOOOOOOOOOOOOO...")

Keema Waterfield

My Sister's a Whale in the Sea

words and music by Nancy Schimmel

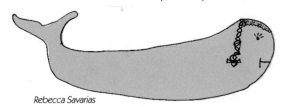

Rebecca Savarias

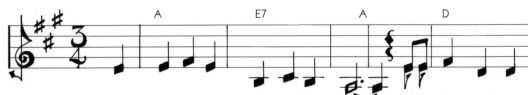

1. My sis- ter's a whale in the sea; I__ don't think she
2. My sis- ter's a whale in the sea; I've a co- py of

knows a- bout me. I like to i- ma- gine her
her pe- di- gree. I picked out a name and my

swim- ming a- round, from Stell- wa- gen Bank__ to Nan- tuck- et
mom sent the cash. It was- n't much money for such a big

Sound. My sis- ter, my sis- ter, my sis- ter's a
splash. My sis- ter, my sis- ter, my sis- ter's a

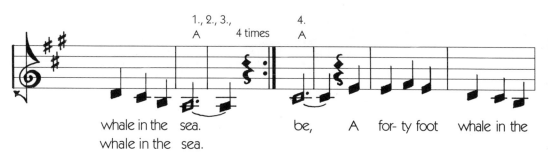

whale in the sea.

whale in the sea.

be, A for-ty foot whale in the

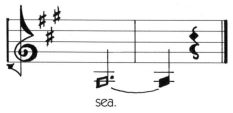

sea.

3. My sister's a whale in the sea,
   Swimming so strong and so free.
   The money will help people learn about whales,
   They know which is whose by the cut of their tails.
   My sister, my sister,
   My sister's a whale in the sea.

4. So look on your family tree.
   Is there room for a humpback or three?
   There's Mirror and Merlin and Clover and Cloud,
   A sister or brother to make you feel proud.
   Your sister, your sister, your sister could very well be,
   A forty-foot whale in the sea.

Performer's Note:
If you'd like to find out about adopting a whale, write:

Whale Adoption Project
320 Gifford Street
Falmouth, Massachusetts 02540

Nobody Else Like Me

words and music by Mary Lu Walker

No- body else in the   world like me!   Nobody else like   ME!

Some- bod- y else may   have my name, but   no- bod- y else is   just the same. There's

no- body else,   no- bo- dy else,   there's   no- bod- y else like   me!

Strongly!   **Return to beginning!**

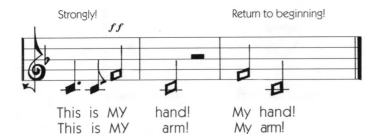

This is MY   hand!   My hand!
This is MY   arm!   My arm!

This is my hand!
This is my arm!
This is my foot!
These are my eyes!
This is my nose!
This is my mouth!
This is my self!

Oh No!
I Like My Sister!

words and music by Barry Louis Polisar

Chorus

Oh no! I like my sis- ter! Oh no, guess you can say I've missed her.

Verse

1. Oh___ my, What am I to do! I
2. We'd al- ways bicker, she'd al- ways fight. She'd

nev- er thought I'd like her, what a- bout you?
always call me wrong, when I knew I was right.

We al- ways ar- gued, she was such a pest. She
She'd steal my cook- ies, she'd grab my cake, I'd say

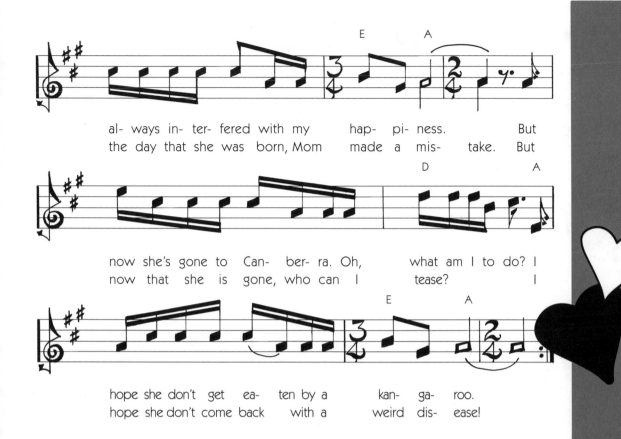

al- ways in- ter- fered with my   hap- pi- ness.   But
the day that she was born, Mom   made a mis- take.   But

now she's gone to Can- ber- ra. Oh,   what am I to do? I
now that she is gone, who can I   tease?   I

hope she don't get ea- ten by a   kan- ga- roo.
hope she don't come back   with a   weird dis- ease!

3. I can't believe I'm saying this! I can't believe my ears;
   This has always been one of my deepest fears.
   I hope that she comes home soon, safe and sound.
   I promise I won't ever hold her upside-down.
   I promise I won't ever put my fingers in her food.
   Nor will I do anything mean or rude.

Read a Book

words and music by Marcy Marxer

1. If you want ad- ven- ture, you want to un- wind,
2. If you've got a ques- tion, some- thing's on your mind.

Pick up a good sto- ry, get out of that old grind, and read a
Read- ing is the an- swer, be a. mas- ter- mind. Read a

book (Read, read, read, read a book.) Read a book. (Read, read,
book. (Read, read, read, read a book.) Read a book. (Read, read,

read, read a book.) If fun is what you're af- ter, or you're
read, read a book.) There is a way to find out,

look- ing for laugh- ter, read a book. (Read, read, read, read a book.)
don't leave an- y doubt, read a book. (Read, read, read, read a book.)

3. Day time, night time, morning time, noon
    Afternoon, bedtime, any time is good to
    Read a book (read, read, read, read a book).
    Read a book (read, read, read, read a book).
    Don't you wear a frown, now, sit right down and
    Read a book (read, read, read, read a book).

4. When it is your bedtime and
    You cannot get to sleep,
    Reading is the answer.
    Why bother counting sheep?
    Read a book (read, read, read, read a book).
    Read a book (read, read, read, read a book).
    Pull the covers round, now
    Snuggle on down and
    Read a book (read, read, read, read a book).

Troy Choquette

Simple Thing

words and music by Jerry Brodey

(Capo up one fret)
Chorus

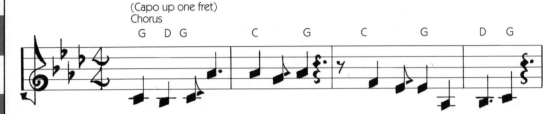

There's a sim- ple thing we do, when we get to- geth- er.

There's a lov- ing thing we do when we share to- geth- er.

1. Home is where I like to be. Spend- ing time with fam-
2. We will see what ques- tions come. And where to find the

i- ly. We are friends, we've come to- geth- er,
an- swers from. There is room to make mis- takes. When

see- ing you gives me so much plea- sure.
I'm with you, I feel so safe.

3. We can do anything we want
   Anything we try.
   When we put our hands together.
   Such a simple thing,
   Such a simple thing we try.

Teaching Peace

words and music by Red and Kathy Grammer

Teach- ing peace all the world a- round. You and me, ev- 'ry

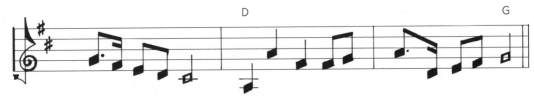

cit- y, ev- 'ry town. One by one, in our work and in our play,

(once the first time, twice each time after)

We are teach- ing peace in what we do and what we say.

(piano interlude first time only)

1. It's up to
2. So take my

us to show we care, reach- ing out to ev- 'ry- bod- y ev- 'ry
hand and come a- long. It's time to sing the world a brand new

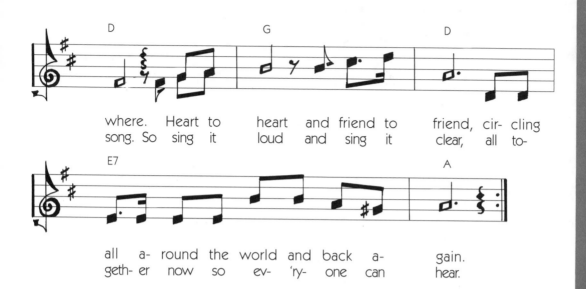

where. Heart to heart and friend to friend, cir- cling
song. So sing it loud and sing it clear, all to-

all a- round the world and back a- gain.
geth- er now so ev- 'ry- one can hear.

Morgan Ramsey-Elliot

Tick Tock

words and music by Linda Arnold

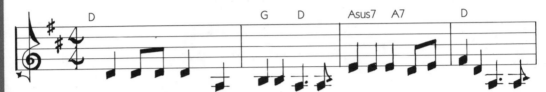

Grand- fa- ther clock stands in the hall. It's ver- y old and it's ve- ry tall and

though it is a state- ly sight, it ne- ver can tell the time just

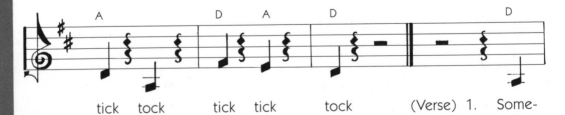

right. And it goes (CHORUS) tick tock

tick tock tick tick tock tick tick tick tick tock

tick tock tick tick tock (Verse) 1. Some-

times it stops, some- times it goes, and just what's wrong, no-

bod- y knows, but ev- 'ry time that I pass by, it al- ways seems to

wink its eye. And it goes. . . 2. Well, mo- ther called the

ex- pert in to see what he could do. He gave it a knock and he

gave it a shake and the clock struck twen- ty

two! And it went . . .

Deedra M. Kinerk

3. Last night I heard the strang- est thing:
first a roar then a ring. When I crept out of my bed, the
clock was stand- ing on its head! And it went. . . 4. This
morn- ing I dis- creet- ly tried to o- pen it and look in- side, but a
voice cried "Ooooh, oh, can't you see? You're tick tock tick tock
tick- l- ing me!" And it went . . . (CHORUS)

The Walrus Life

words and music by Bill Wellington

Chorus
D   G   A7   D   G   A7

Oh, the wal- rus life is real- ly grand, way up north in the Arc- tic land, with

D   G   Em   A7   D   A7   D

all my friends, and my fam- i- ly, oh, the wal- rus life is the life for me!

Final Chorus   Verse
A7   G   A7   D

wal- rus life is the life for me!____   1. Well, I'm
                                           2. When____

D   G   A7   D   G   A

not a fish and I'm not a snail, not a tur- tle and I'm not a whale. I'm a
I go down to the sea to swim, I flap my tail__ and I flip my fins. I____

wal- rus and you know it's true that I real- ly don't look a lot like you!
swim a- bout most

ev- 'ry- where, and now and then I come up for air___

___. Oh, the

3. Well, I don't mind the snow and ice,
   In fact, I think they're really nice.
   I can swim about in a winter storm,
   'Cause I got a lot of blubber to keep
   me warm!

What Happened to the Dinosaurs?

words and music by Paul Strausman

What hap- pened to the di- no- saurs? Where did they go? Was it

hun- ger, the cold, did they just grow old? I guess we'll ne- ver know, no,

no, no. I guess we'll ne- ver know_____.

2. There's a

1. Ma- ny years a- go when the earth was much young- er, and there
Bron- to- saur- us, Tri- cera- tops, Ty- ran- no- saur- us Rex _____,

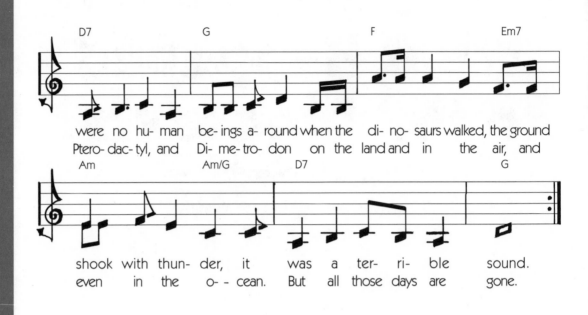

were no hu- man | be- ings a- round when the | di- no- saurs walked, the ground
Ptero- dac- tyl, and | Di- me- tro- don | on the land and in | the air, and

shook with thun- der, it | was a ter- ri- ble | sound.
even in the o- - cean. | But all those days are | gone.

3. Now fossils and tracks are all they left behind
   To tell us of the past.
   It's been millions of years since the passing of the dinosaurs.
   It all went by so fast.

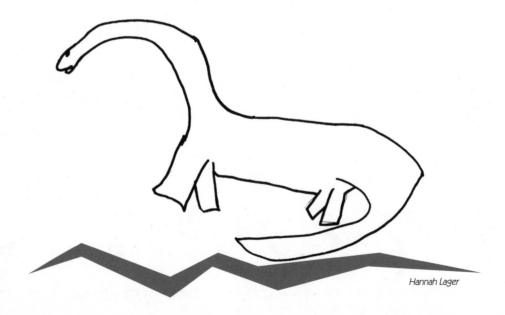

Hannah Lager

The World Is a Rainbow

words and music by Greg Scelsa

The world is a rain- - bow___ ___ that's filled with man- y col- ors___. Yel- low, black and white, and brown, you see them all a- - - round. The world is a rain- - - bow ___, with man- y kinds of peo- ple___
(2. La la la)

____. It takes all kinds of peo- ple to make the world go 'round.

1., 2. Now you be you, and I'll be me. That's the

way we were meant to be____. But the world is a mix- ing cup, just

look what hap- pens when you stir it up.

The world is a rain- bow ____, with many kinds of

peo- ple ____, and when we work to- - - geth- er, it's such a sight to

see.   The world is   beau- ti- ful when we   live in har- mo- – – ny.___

La _____ la la la la

ny.___.   La, la, la, etc.

Luke Boyles

The Artists . . .

Timmy Abell

North Carolina folk singer/storyteller Timmy Abell draws on a repertoire of music brimming with character, humor, and tradition. A versatile artist, Timmy switches from one early American instrument to another with the ease of a thorough professional. From hammered to Appalachian dulcimer, the bowed psaltery to banjo, concertina, and penny whistle, Timmy introduces young people to a wide range of musical styles and instruments. On his recording *The Farmer's Market,* Timmy introduces five of his original children's songs with a fine mix of contemporary and traditional favorites.

> Upstream Records
> Box 8843, Asheville, North Carolina 28814
> 704-258-9713

Peter Alsop

Peter Alsop is a singer/songwriter/humorist from southern California who is noted for his warmth and insight. Peter uses music and humor to address subjects most people find hard to talk about, and he sings them in a healing way. His songs are used by thousands of parents, educators, and human service professionals to help families and others discuss sensitive issues. Peter sees through the eyes of children and writes humorous songs celebrating human values. He has a Ph.D. in Educational Psychology and travels across the country, not only performing, but lecturing as well. Kids and parents laugh and learn healthy ideas about self-esteem, open-mindedness, self-protection, and much, much more!

> Moose School Productions
> Box 960, Topanga, California 95560
> 800-676-5480

Linda Arnold

Linda Arnold's musical world is filled with enchanting and magical songs that paint pictures of clocks that talk, cows that squawk, and lonely vegetables that lament because kids won't eat them. Linda encourages children to exercise their imagination, to "see" her songs, and to add to the songs in their own inventive ways. Whether she is singing about loving pizza, learning math, respecting living creatures, or the need for peace in the world, Linda's songs harmonize with children's experiences and fantasies. Linda lives in Santa Cruz, California, with her two children, Katy and Toby, and hosts the nationally syndicated radio program *Pickleberry Pie*.

> A & M Records
> 1416 N. La Brea Avenue, Hollywood, California 90028
> 800-888-5301

Kim and Jerry Brodey

With their combined backgrounds rooted in education, music, midwifery, and theatrical performance, Kim and Jerry are committed to children's culture. They divide their time between creating songs, artwork, producing records and videos, and staying in touch with the issues and events in the world around them. The Brodeys are a blended family living in Toronto with Kim's children, Joshua and Oliver. Together they are the focus of an award-winning documentary film called *Step Dancing: Portrait of a Remarried Family*. Kim and Jerry continue to work their musical magic on thousands of children, parents, and teachers across Canada and the United States.

> Kids' Entertainment
> 204-A St. George Street, Toronto, Ontario,
> Canada M5R 2N6

Tom Callinan

Tom Callinan's musical ability and inventive compositions have fashioned his recognition as the celebrated Connecticut Troubadour. As a balladeer, composer, and performer on a score of instruments, Tom is a multi-faceted artist. In addition to his many performances, Tom has appeared on *Good Morning, America* and *Shining Time Station*. Two of his original compositions were included in an Emmy-Award-winning documentary produced by Connecticut Public Television. He has presented programs from Maine to Florida, including at The John F. Kennedy Center for the Performing Arts in Washington, D.C.

> Crackerbarrel Entertainments
> 168 Shore Road, Clinton, Connecticut 06413
> 203-669-6581

The Chenille Sisters

The Chenille Sisters forayed into children's music at the suggestion of their record company, Red House Records: "We talked about what we liked and disliked about children's music, listening to a lot of stuff, and then started writing and looking for material." The result is a great selection of their own original songs and other material. Connie Huber, Cheryl Dawdy, and Grace Morand combine fine vocals, rich harmonies, and a sense of whimsy that have become Chenille trademarks: "More than parenthood, what's crucial to the creation of good kids' music is a recollection of one's own kidhood," and the Chenille Sisters certainly have plenty of that.

> Red House Records
> Box 4044, St. Paul, Minnesota 55104
> 612-379-1089

Jonathan Edwards

Born in Minnesota, Jonathan Edwards first learned music from his grandmother, who wrote hymns and gospel tunes. He studied art in college but music soon won out as his favorite form of self-expression. In the late 1960s, he moved to Boston with the band Sugar Creek, then launched a solo career. Jonathan's vocal and harmonica skills can also be heard on recordings by Emmylou Harris, Tom Rush, Bill Staines, and Jimmy Buffet. *Little Hands,* Jonathan's recording of "songs for and about children," is perhaps his warmest and most sincere, and will surely delight old fans and win many new young followers.

> American Melody Records
> Box 270, Guilford, Connecticut 06437
> 203-457-0881

Cathy Fink and Marcy Marxer

Yabbadabbadoo! Cathy Fink and Marcy Marxer have been entertaining kids and adults since 1974. Whether they are singing, songwriting, or making homemade musical instruments, Cathy and Marcy know how to have fun. They created their most recent children's album, *Help Yourself,* to encourage self-reliance and self-empowerment. They've also made two videos: *Making and Playing Homemade Instruments* and *Kid's Guitar,* which have received rave reviews. If you are lucky enough to see them in concert, you can expect great singing, speed-yodeling, some slap-cheek playing, and maybe some cowgirl rope tricks!

> Rounder Records
> One Camp Street, Cambridge, Massachusetts 02140
> 800-44-DISCS

Marc and Carol Finkelstein

Marc and Carol are two creative and skilled musicians with a background common to many composers of children's music: each has training in music and education. Marc has degrees from Berklee College of Music and Rutgers University. Carol has received degrees from Boston Conservatory of Music and Georgian Court College. Together they have several albums, including *Everyday's a Holiday,* a collection of upbeat songs about holidays celebrated by American school children, and *Meet the Beat,* a recording of innovative songs featuring rhythm and movement activities for preschool and primary elementary kids.

> Melody House, Inc.
> 819 N.W. 92nd Street, Oklahoma City, Oklahoma 73114
> 800-234-9228

Red Grammer

Red Grammer's music and performances make people feel great. He's energetic, positive, a spectacular singer, and a gifted performer. In 1981, Red replaced Glen Yarborough in the famous folk group The Limelighters. Shortly after that, Red and his wife Kathy became interested in children's music. In 1983, they released their children's cassette, *Can You Sound Just Like Me?,* which was so successful that he began performing children's music and resigned from the Limelighters. Red recorded his classic record *Teaching Peace* to help children and their parents "break down the 'big' idea of world peace into individual daily activities that will make it a reality."

> Smilin' Atcha Music
> 81-B Sugarloaf Mountain Road,
> Chester, New York 10918
> 914-469-9450

Greg and Steve

What is the one word that most accurately describes the music of Greg Scelsa and Steve Mellang? FUN! Greg and Steve offer all-original songs inspired by greats like Cab Calloway and boogie-down, kiddie-style! If you're wondering how funky these guys can be, you should know that they have produced for the Temptations. And they bring that beat to their kids' activity songs, which encourage children to participate, to succeed without competition, and to feel good about themselves.

> Youngheart Records
> Box 27784, Los Angeles, California 90027
> 213-663-3223

Bill Harley

Bill Harley has won acclaim across the country for his unique blend of songs and stories, entertaining children and adults alike. Whether he is singing the songs from *Fifty Ways to Fool Your Mother, You're in Trouble,* or *In the Hospital* (with Peter Alsop), Bill's sparkling songs and stories leave listeners with a feeling of having learned a valuable lesson without having to endure a lecture. In addition to recording eight albums, Bill narrated and wrote the songs on an award-winning film series by Learning Tree Films. He grows a large garden at his home in Seekonk, Massachusetts, with the help of his wife, Debbie Block, and two sons, Noah and Dylan.

> Round River Records
> 301 Jacob Street, Seekonk, Massachusetts 02771
> 508-336-9703

Eric Hummel and Peggy Hovik

On their new release, singers Eric Hummel and Peggy Hovik write and sing *Soggy Songs of Southeast Alaska.* Whether they are singing about octopus, peanut butter jellyfish, fishing with Dad, or sailing softly to bed, their acoustic arrangements make this a tape that children love and parents enjoy (even when played over and over). Though the songs are uniquely Alaskan, their lyrics will appeal to anyone who enjoys living and playing outdoors. Eric and Peggy live in Ketchikan, Alaska, where they raise their families on fresh salmon, fresh bread, fresh rainwater, and, of course, fresh music.

> Clam Cove Music
> Box 5736, Ketchikan, Alaska 99901
> 907-225-0800

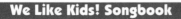

Ella Jenkins

is perhaps the most influential children's performer in American music. Since her first television appearances in Chicago in 1956, Ella has been performing for children throughout the world. Ella's innovative "call-and-response" method actively encourages children's participation, and her use of music from diverse cultures has made her an important figure in multicultural education. Ella's outstanding reputation in the field of children's music has led to her being referred to as "the First Lady of the children's folk song."

> Smithsonian/Folkways Records
> One Camp Street, Cambridge, Massachusetts 02140
> 800-346-4445

Jory

Jory is a childhood music specialist. Music has always been an important part of her life. Jory started guitar lessons at eight and later learned to play the mandolin. She sings about dogs and cats, mud, clouds, old creaky houses, and bubbles. "I don't like to patronize children or sing down to them. I've worked with children long enough to know what they'll respond to. . . . I like to sing about real things." In addition to children's concerts, Jory has started performing for mentally handicapped teens and adults, and she gives workshops to teachers on how to do "active music" with children. Her cassette releases include *Fruit Salad, Beans for Brunch,* and *Duck Lips.*

> Aronsound
> Box 3004-183, Corvallis, Oregon 97339
> 503-754-9493

Saragail Katzman

Saragail Katzman comes to children's songwriting/performing with a strong background in musical theater. She has performed off-off-Broadway and in New York City cabarets. Saragail wrote the music, lyrics, and libretto for two musicals, *The Furnished Room* and *The Alexandria Municipal Reading Library,* which have been produced by theater companies all over the United States. Saragail believes, "Everybody's got music!" Her original songs encourage listeners to get up, get active, and get into creative movement using lots of fantasy. She has performed her one-woman children's show, *A Joyful Noise!,* throughout New York, and it is now available on cassette.

> A Joyful Noise
> 209-10 41st Avenue, #3-0, Bayside, New York, 11361
> 718-279-3624

Lois LaFond

Lois LaFond likes to make music with her friends in the band The Rockadiles, because they play all kinds of music. From African rhythms to reggae, rock and roll, salsa, the blues, and more, Lois's music is truly international. As pianist George Winston says, "Her music does not need to be simplified for kids. It just works! . . . The blend is uncluttered and refreshing." Lois's vitality, sense of humor, and global philosophy can all be heard in her music. As she explains, "In an era when the world is becoming smaller, we need to begin to connect with each other. Music . . . language . . . art all work that way." So do the music and stories of Lois LaFond.

> Lois LaFond & Company
> Box 4712, Boulder, Colorado 80306
> 303-444-7095

Carol Lavrakas

Carol Lavrakas produced *Children's Songs of the Midnight Sun* (Volumes I and II), which have become two of the best-selling cassettes produced in the state of Alaska. Proceeds from sales of the cassettes are donated to child-abuse prevention efforts in the 49th state. Through the music in Volume I, children learn the months of the year, the importance of finishing school, and how to say "I love you" in Tlingit, a Native language of Southeast Alaska. Volume II features a Russian children's song, an Irish jig, a French dance, and ten more original songs. Their music has been praised by the National Association for the Education of Young Children and the Children's Television Workshop, the producers of Sesame Street.

> Ageless Music Works
> Box 91344, Anchorage, Alaska 99509
> 907-248-0877

Tom Paxton

During his long career, Tom Paxton has written four books, recorded twenty-nine albums, and performed thousands of memorable concerts for countless fans throughout the world. He has written many songs that have become classics, including "The Marvelous Toy," "The Last Thing on My Mind," and "Jennifer's Rabbit." He has released seven children's recordings and five children's books. As one reviewer wrote, "Paxton can turn out incredibly funny songs . . .(and) craft lyrics so simple and perfect that they become part of the oral tradition within a few years." Whether his songs are written for children or for adults, his music is always compelling.

> Pax Records
> 78 Park Place, East Hampton, New York 11937

Peanutbutterjam

The ingredients for Peanutbutterjam are Eileen Packard on accordion and Paul Recker on guitar. Eileen has been a primary-grade teacher in Hartford, Connecticut, for over 15 years. Multi-talented in art, music, writing, and performing, she has an amazing gift for communicating with young people. Paul Recker, a sensitive, energetic, and versatile performer, has been bringing his special musical talents to audiences for over 20 years, in concert and through his recordings. They have been performing as Peanutbutterjam since 1980, captivating young audiences with a fanciful blend of music, storytelling, and puppetry.

> Peanutbutterjam
> Box 2687, Hartford, Connecticut 06146-2687
> 203-871-1268

Barry Louis Polisar

WARNING: Barry Louis Polisar is dangerous. Exposure might result in a sense of humor. Children are advised to use discretion when exposing grown-ups to his books and recordings. Alias "Shel Silverstein with hair," Barry plays guitar, writes songs and books, and is heard regularly on numerous radio and TV shows. Tormented babysitters, pesky sisters, and bothersome brothers inhabit Barry's musical world. His humorous songs about the more unruly pleasures of childhood will have your children giggling and will even bring a smile to your face. As one listener reports, "We all remember our childhood . . . and Barry Louis Polisar wants to make sure we don't forget it."

> Rainbow Morning Music
> 2121 Fairland Road, Silver Spring, Maryland 20904
> 301-384-9207

The Singing Rainbows

The Singing Rainbows are an award-winning singing group of young people ranging in age from 11 to 17. Under the direction of Candy Forest, The Singing Rainbows have two critically acclaimed recordings, *All In This Together—15 Ecology Songs for the Whole Family,* and *Head First and Belly Down.* Specializing in "music that makes a difference," the group has performed for the United Nations 45th Birthday Party, The San Francisco Zoo, The Coyote Point Environmental Habitat Center, the Lindsay Museum of National History, and school and library concerts. Their ecology club, ARK (Association of Rainbow Kids), has members as far away as Europe and Africa.

> Sisters' Choice
> 1450 Sixth Street, Berkeley, California 94710
> 510-843-0533

Willie Sterba

Willie Sterba's first song was a love song for Diane, his college sweetheart. Marriage came four years later, followed by a move to California, where they both taught school. At first, music was secondary to his teaching career, but Willie soon began writing songs for his own children and performing in local libraries and schools. The family moved back to Mineral Point, Wisconsin, in 1986 to begin Singing Toad Productions. Today Willie has three recordings for children, a busy performing career, and a weekly radio show, "Dancing Dog Radio." The whole family—Diane as The Story Lady and Senora Lenora, and daughters Anika, age 9, as Rita Rocket Roving Reporter, and Katrina, age 6, as The Joke Buglett—takes part in the fun.

> Singing Toad Productions
> Box 359, Mineral Point, Wisconsin 53565
> 608-987-2224

Paul Strausman

Paul Strausman is a musician, songwriter, and educator whose finger is on the pulse of the playground set. His uncomplicated songs address the everyday concerns of childhood, such as losing a tooth, fear of the dark, or moving to a new town. They provide information in a fun way that is genuinely useful to children. In addition to performing and recording, Paul teaches workshops on songwriting, instrument building, and special topics (American history, social change, and the environment). Paul discovered the rewards of performing for children through Ruth Pelham's innovative "Music Mobile" program, and he's been hooked ever since.

> A Gentle Wind
> Box 3103, Albany, New York 12203
> 518-436-0391

Nancy Tucker

There's a language only kids understand . . . kids and Nancy Tucker. She's fluent in the rhymes and rhythms and word-flips and somersaults that get kids stomping their feet and singing along. Nancy is the recipient of several awards, including Connecticut Songwriter of the Year, and is one of the top guitarists in New England. A songwriter with four albums to her credit, she travels the country performing original comedy and songs for people of all ages.

> A Gentle Wind
> Box 3103, Albany, New York 12203
> 518-436-0391

J. D. Uponen and Lori Pleshe

After their marriage in 1983, J. D. Uponen and Lori Pleshe-Uponen found themselves making the journey from their home in Michigan to Kenai, Alaska. After three years, Lori left her teaching job to care for the couple's newborn daughter. J. D. continued to teach music and compose songs. They recorded their first children's tape, *Brown Bear Boogie,* in 1987. The tape's success led them to create a second tape, *Polar Bear Polka,* in 1990. Meanwhile, the success of their first child led them to produce another. J. D. jokes, "Now we have all four parts covered!" Lori and J. D. enjoy their kids and hope you enjoy their tapes.

> Mooma Music
> Box 2141, Kenai, Alaska 99611
> 907-283-3141

Jim Valley

Jim Valley's young fans have never heard of the band Paul Revere and the Raiders, but their parents have. Now the former guitarist for the band is singing about friendship, butterflies, and a brontosaurus named Morris, much to the delight of his present-day fans. In his Rainbow Planet Workshops, children create song lyrics and Jim sets their words to music. "I want to help keep the creative child in them alive and well," he says. "The heart of children contains a wealth of creativity and wisdom." Jim's four albums are dedicated to the spirit of friendship, and he spreads that message in Rainbow Planet concerts across the country and around the world.

> Rainbow Planet
> 5110 Cromwell Drive, Gig Harbor, Washington 98335
> 206-265-3758

Mary Lu Walker

Composer, performer, and songwriter for the child in all of us, Mary Lu Walker brings humor and originality to the age-old message of peace on earth. She sings songs of laughter, of the pleasure of living, of personal dignity, and of hope. "Children, especially, need a gentleness in their lives," Mary Lu explains. "They need to feel there is hope, because they get a lot of unhopeful messages." Mary Lu has performed in countries on five continents, including the former USSR, Fiji, and Japan. Her songs delight people of all ages with their universal appeal. "Nobody Else Like Me" is from her latest cassette entitled, *Frog's Party.*

> A Gentle Wind
> Box 3103, Albany, New York 12203
> 518-436-0391

Bill Wellington

Bill Wellington is the creator of "Radio WOOF," which began as a school intercom "radio" broadcast from the WOrld Of Folklore and became the central concept behind an award-winning children's recording. Through storytelling, traditional and contemporary music, funny songs, and dialogue with a zany cast of characters, Wellington introduces Irish flute, collects family folklore, calls square dances, and performs extensively for school-age and family audiences throughout the country.

> Well-In-Tune Productions
> 719 Churchville Avenue, Staunton, Virginia 24401
> 703-885-0233

Resources . . .

Music

A & M Records
1416 North La Brea Avenue
Hollywood, California 90028

A Gentle Wind
Box 3103
Albany, New York 12203

Alacazam!
Box 429
Waterbury, Vermont 05676

American Melody
Box 270
Guilford, Connecticut 06437

Children's Music Network
Box 307
Montvale, New Jersey
07645-0307
Attn: Andrea Stone

Educational Activities
Box 392
Freeport, New York 11520

Elephant Records
Box 101, Station Z
Toronto, Ontario,
Canada M5N 2Z3

Flying Fish Records
1304 West Schubert
Chicago, Illinois 60614

Kimbo Educational
Box 477
Long Branch, New Jersey 07740

Ladyslipper
Box 3124
Durham, North Carolina 27705

Music for Little People
Box 1460
Redway, California 95560

Red House Records
Box 4044
St. Paul, Minnesota 55104

Rhino Records
2225 Colorado Blvd.
Santa Monica, California 90404

Rhythms Productions
Box 34485
Los Angeles, California 90034-0485

Rounder Records
One Camp Street
Cambridge, Massachusetts 02140

Walt Disney Records
500 South Buena Vista Street
Burbank, California 91521

Waterlily Music
333 West Maplewood Crescent
Milton, Ontario, Canada L9T 2G7

Storytelling

E.A.R.S. Storytelling Center
12019 Donohue Avenue
Louisville, Kentucky 40242

N.A.P.P.S.
(National Organization for the
Preservation and Perpetuation of
Storytelling)
Box 309
Jonesborough, Tennessee
37659-9983

Weston Woods
Weston, Connecticut 06683

Books

All Ears by Jill Jarnow
Viking/Penguin Books

Magazines

Copycat
Box 081546
Racine, Wisconsin 53408

Folksong in the Classroom
229 Suffolk Street
Holyoke, Massachusetts 01040

Music K-8
Plank Road Publishing
12237 Watertown Plank Road
Box 26627
Wauwatosa, Wisconsin 53226

SING OUT!
Box 5253
Bethlehem, Pennsylvania 18015

Syndicated Radio Programs

Dancing Dog Radio
Willie Sterba
Box 359
Mineral Point, Wisconsin 53565

Kids Alive!
Jamie Deming
Children's Radio Productions
Northern Boulevard
East Norwich, New York 11732

Pickleberry Pie
P. J. Swift
305 Dickens Way
Santa Cruz, California 95604

WE LIKE KIDS!
Jeff and Judy
KTOO-FM
224 Fourth Street
Juneau, Alaska 99801

Lael Harrison